Friends
(Mostly)

By **Barbara Joosse**

Illustrated by
Tomaso Milian

Greenwillow Books
An Imprint of HarperCollinsPublishers

Friends (Mostly)
Text copyright © 2010 by Barbara Joosse
Illustrations copyright © 2010 by Tomaso Milian
All rights reserved. Manufactured in China.
For information address HarperCollins Children's Books,
a division of HarperCollins Publishers,
10 East 53rd Street, New York, NY 10022.
www.harpercollinschildrens.com

Watercolors were used to prepare the full-color art.
The text type is 20-point Futura Medium.

Library of Congress Cataloging-in-Publication Data

Joosse, Barbara.
Friends (mostly) / by Barbara Joosse ; illustrated by Tomaso Milian.
p. cm.
"Greenwillow Books."
Summary: Henry and Ruby are best friends forever,
even though they do not always get along.
ISBN 978-0-06-088221-1 (trade bdg.) — ISBN 978-0-06-088222-8 (lib. bdg.)
[1. Best friends—Fiction. 2. Friendship—Fiction.] I. Milian, Tomaso, ill. II. Title.
PZ7.J7435Fri 2010   [E]—dc22   2009034951

10 11 12 13 14 SCP 10 9 8 7 6 5 4 3 2 1
First Edition
Greenwillow Books

For Mary Ackerman, sister and friend
—B. J.

Alla mamma e al papá, con amore
—T. M.

Ruby and Henry,
Henry and Ruby.
Usually we're friends,
but sometimes we're unfriends.

It all depends.

Ruby: For Henry's birthday, I give him something he really wants, like a fake nose and mustache, and not a coloring book.

I cry at his pet funerals.
I split my Nutty-Bar
so it comes out even.

Henry: For Ruby's birthday, I give her lipstick because that is her favorite.
I let her peel the nose off my banana.
I never open her secret box.

Henry: In circus, I'm the ringmaster and Ruby's the lion tamer.

We're both the Amazing Suspendas,
who perform on the flying trapeze.

Ruby: In pirates, I dig for buried treasure and Henry keeps an eye peeled for Scurvy Dog Sam.

Then Henry gets the gold doubloons
and I get all the rubies.

These things are a very good trade.

Ruby: But at swimming lessons, Henry did the dead man's float.

All I could do was dead man. "Wow," somebody said. "Ruby sinks like a stone."

So I splashed Henry's towel
accidentally on purpose.

"Cut it out," he sputtered.
"Serves you right," I muttered.
Who wants to be friends with a show-off?

Ruby: Anyway, there are a million things to do when you're an Only.

Puzzles. Bug watching. Marching. Whatever you want. I picked marching. Of course, I wore boots with silver spangles. I marched and drummed and drummed and marched

and blew my whistle
—*wheeeeet!*
—in front of Henry's house.
I did a twirligig and then . . .

Henry: . . . I fell in behind her.
"What are you doing?" she asked.
"I'm being the rest of the parade," I said,
"so you can be the leader."

Oh, Ruby is the fancy one,
the dancy prancy chancy one.
She twizzles like sparklers
    and fireflies
    and bracelets.
Sometimes she's bossy,
but she has ideas you usually
    want to do.
This is why
she is my
BEST FRIEND!

Oh, Henry is the sturdy one,
the zurly burly worry one.
I can always count on Henry—
    like a tree
    and peanut butter
    and purple.
Sometimes he's a 'fraidy,
but he almost always
    does things anyway.
This is why
he is my
BEST FRIEND!

Henry: Last night, I had worry thoughts.
What if Ruby finds another best friend?
Nothing would be funny. Nothing would be regular.

What would I do without Ruby?

Ruby: Yesterday, I had gruffly thoughts.
That Henry won't do what I want! That Henry can ride without training wheels! That Henry got the biggest half! But then I think . . .

What would I do without Henry?

Henry: I said to Ruby I'm afraid of the dark and I sleep with a bear and I call him Weddy Teddy.

And then she told!

Ruby: But only one single person.

Ruby: I said to Henry that I like Simon, that he has curls on his head like little buttons and I want to poke my finger in and make one *sproing*.

He told my secret . . .
to a *boy!*

Henry: What's wrong
with that? I'm a boy.

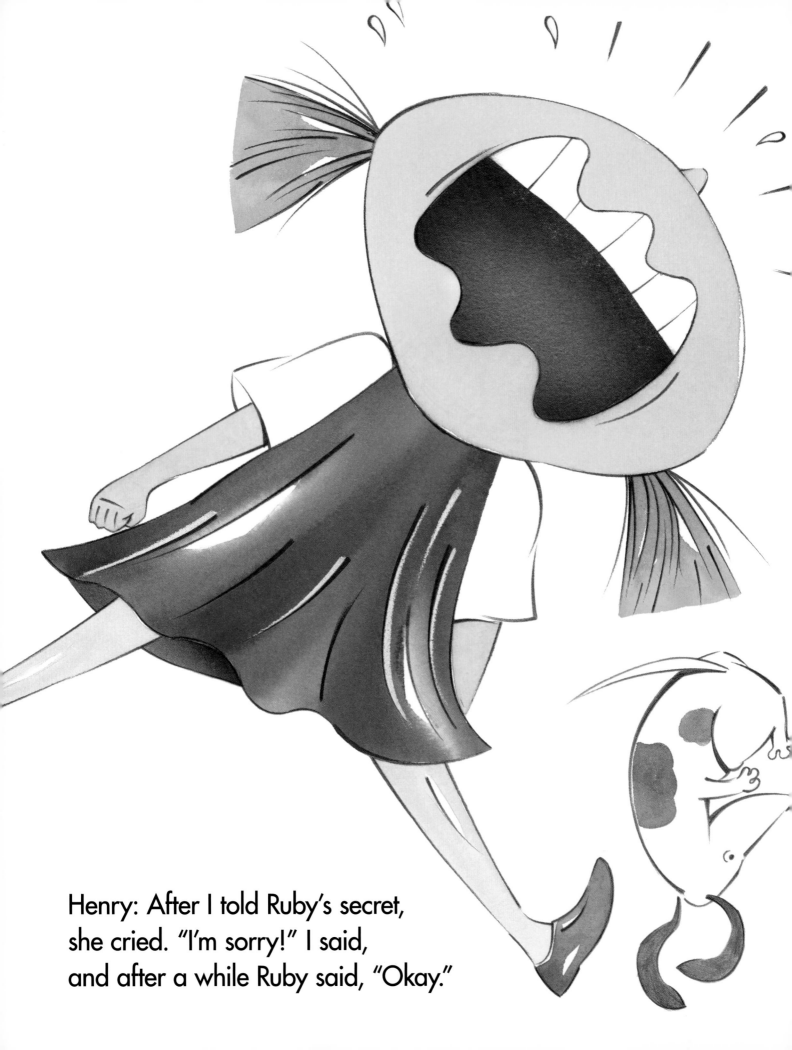

Henry: After I told Ruby's secret,
she cried. "I'm sorry!" I said,
and after a while Ruby said, "Okay."

Ruby: After I told Henry's secret, his face got red. "I'm sorry," I said. *Really* sorry." After a while Henry said, "Okay."

Henry and Ruby—usually friends,
but sometimes unfriends.
RubyandHenry go together
for always and forever

like mashed and potatoes
like bellies and buttons
like piggy and back.

NOT the end.